DOGS DON'T DO

Ballet

For Amber, James, Lauren, and Isaac, with love—A. K.

For Michael (believer in Biff)—S. O.

SIMON & SCHUSTER BOOKS FOR YOUNG READERS
An imprint of Simon & Schuster Children's Publishing Division
1230 Avenue of the Americas, New York, New York 10020
Text copyright © 2010 by Anna Kemp
Illustrations copyright © 2010 by Sara Ogilvie
First published in Great Britain in 2010 by Simon & Schuster UK Ltd.
Published by arrangement with Simon & Schuster UK Ltd.
First US edition 2010
SIMON & SCHUSTER BOOKS FOR YOUNG READERS is a trademark of Simon & Schuster, Inc.
For information about special discounts for bulk purchases, please contact
Simon & Schuster Special Sales at 1-866-506-1949 or business@simonandschuster.com.
The Simon & Schuster Speakers Bureau can bring authors to your live event. For more information or to book an event,
contact the Simon & Schuster Speakers Bureau at 1-866-248-3049 or visit our website at www.simonspeakers.com.
The text for this book is set in Burin.
Manufactured in China / 0615 SUK
4 6 8 10 9 7 5 3
CIP data for this book is available from the Library of Congress.
ISBN 978-1-4169-9839-6

DOGS DON'T DO
Ballet

Anna Kemp
Illustrated by Sara Ogilvie

SIMON & SCHUSTER BOOKS FOR YOUNG READERS

NEW YORK   LONDON   TORONTO   SYDNEY

My dog is not like other dogs.

He doesn't do dog stuff like weeing on fire hydrants,
or scratching his fleas, or drinking out of the toilet.

If I throw him a stick,

he looks at me like I'm crazy.

So I have to fetch it myself.

No, my dog likes music and moonlight and walking on his tiptoes.

You see, my dog doesn't think he's a dog . . .

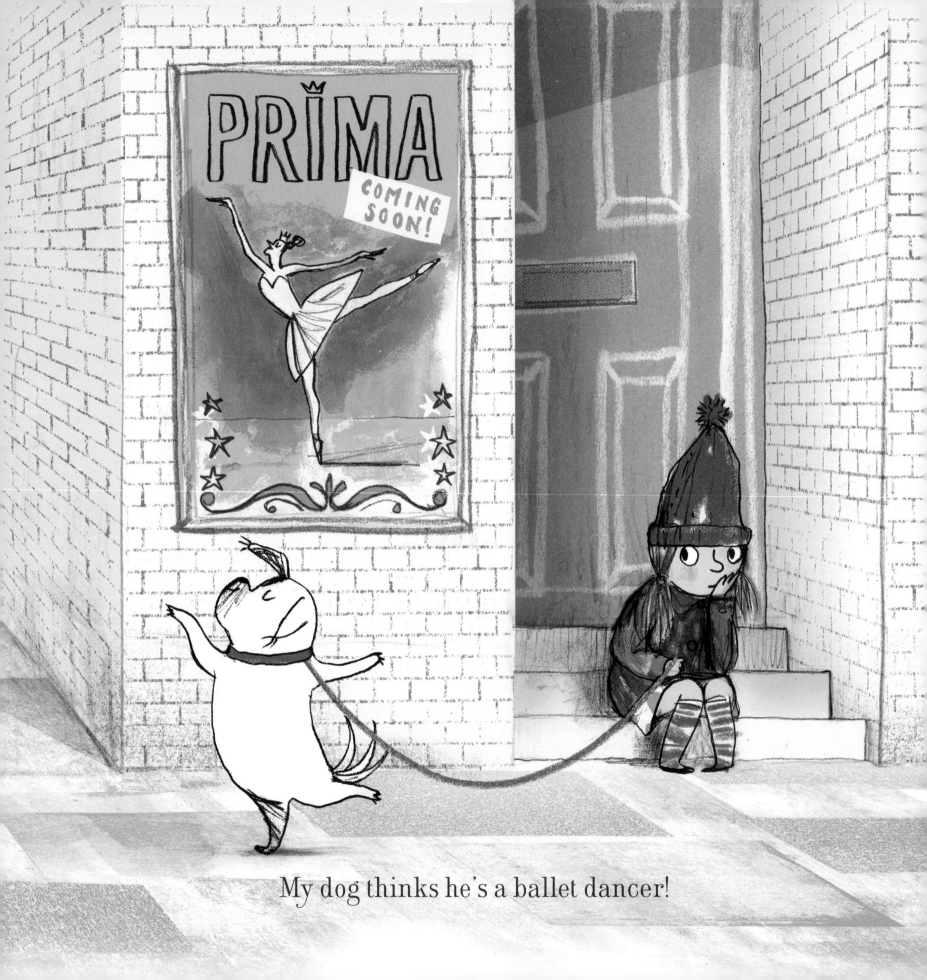

My dog thinks he's a ballet dancer!

When I get ready for ballet class, he looks longingly at my tutu and ballet shoes and I just know he is dreaming of his name in lights.

"Dad," I say, "can Biff come too? He loves ballet."
"Not a chance," says Dad. "Dogs don't do ballet!"

Then, one Saturday on my way to class, I get a funny feeling. A funny feeling that I am being watched. A funny feeling that I am being followed.

When Miss Polly is teaching us a new routine, I think I see something peeking in the window. Something with a wet nose. Something with a tail.

"Okay, girls," says Miss Polly. "Who's going to demonstrate first position?"

But, before any of the girls can step forward, there is a
loud bark from the back of the studio and something
furry rushes to the front.
"What is this?" asks Miss Polly, peering over her glasses.
"This," I say, "is my dog."

"Well, take it away at once," says Miss Polly,
wrinkling up her nose. "Dogs don't do ballet!"
My poor dog stops wagging his tail, and
his ears droop down at the ends.

I take my dog home and give him a bowl of
Doggie Donuts. But he won't touch them.

He just stays in his house for days and
days, and at night he howls at the moon.

For my birthday I get tickets for the Royal Ballet.
"Can Biff come too?" I ask Dad. "He loves ballet."
My dog pricks up his ears and wags his tail.

"No," says Dad. "If I've told you once,
I've told you a thousand times: Dogs don't do ballet!"

As we wait for the bus, I think about my
poor old dog, all on his own, howling at the moon.
Then I get a funny feeling.

A funny feeling that I am being watched.

A funny feeling that I am not alone.

The ballet is magical!
The orchestra plays as the prima ballerina dances
and prances, and twirls and whirls, and skips and . . .

Oh, no! She trips! Disaster! Calamity!
It's all over! I think.

But somebody doesn't think it is over. No, somebody thinks it is just beginning. Somebody with big black eyes, somebody with pointy ears, somebody . . .

... wearing my tutu!

The audience gasps.
"It's a dog!" someone shouts.
"Dogs don't do ballet!"

My dog turns bright red and looks at his feet.
"That's what I've always said," Dad mutters.
But then the orchestra starts to play . . .

. . . and Biff dances like no dog
has ever danced before.
Plié! Jeté! Arabesque! Pirouette!

He is as light as a sugarpuff!
As pretty as a fairy!
The audience can't believe it.
"Hooray!" I shout. "That's my dog!"

When the music stops, my dog
gives a hopeful curtsey and blinks
nervously into the spotlight. The theater is
so very quiet that you could hear a bubble pop.

Then the lady in the front row stands up.
"It's a dog!" she shouts.
Biff's ears start to droop again.

"A dog that does ballet!" she adds. "Bravo!"
Suddenly the whole audience cheers and throws
bunches of roses. My dog glows pink with happiness.
"I don't believe it," says Dad, shaking his head.
"Biff IS a ballet dancer after all!"
"See?" I say proudly, ruffling Biff's ears.
"Dogs DO do ballet. Bravo, Biff!"